THE ADVENTURES OF MARSHALL & ART

Writing a Wrong

by Noel Gyro Potter
illustrated by Joseph Cannon

magic
wagon

visit us at www.abdopublishing.com

To my guys, you always right all of my wrongs. With you, I found a mother's unconditional love.—NGP

Printed in the United States of America, North Mankato, Minnesota.
102009
012010

 PRINTED ON RECYCLED PAPER

Text by Noel Gyro Potter
Illustrated by Joseph Cannon
Edited by Stephanie Hedlund and Rochelle Baltzer
Cover and interior design by Neil Klinepier

Library of Congress Cataloging-in-Publication Data

Potter, Noel Gyro.
  Writing a wrong / by Noel Gyro Potter ; illustrated by Joseph Cannon.
    p. cm. -- (The adventures of Marshall & Art)
  ISBN 978-1-60270-739-9
  [1. Graffiti--Fiction.] I. Cannon, Joseph, 1958- ill. II. Title.
  PZ7.P8553Wr 2009
  [E]--dc22
                    2009038532

Marshall and Art babysat their little brother, Harley, most of the day for their mom. They also fed their cats, Kata and Kumite, and walked their dog, Rocket. They even tidied up the house as a surprise.

When Marti came home from running her errands, she was so pleased, she felt Marshall and Art earned a small reward.

3

Marti gave the boys some money for a movie and some treats. Then, she dropped them off early enough to check out the mall before the show started.

"Stay together and out of trouble, you two. Have a good time!" Marti called out as she made her way out of the busy parking lot.

The boys were strolling around the mall, when Marshall recognized a new boy from school. "Hey there's Nero Stomel!" said Marshall. "He's from France, and I hear he's an amazing artist. He's way cool, too! Hurry, Art, let's catch up to him. Hey, Nero!"

Art struggled a bit to keep up with Marshall.

Nero wasn't sure, but he thought he heard someone call his name from the crowd. Searching for a familiar face, he spotted Marshall.

"Hey, Marshall, what's up? Pretty outrageous mall, huh?" Nero asked.

Marshall was glad that Nero remembered him. "Yeah, we're going to the movies. Nero, this is my younger brother, Art."

"Hey, Art, how ya' doing? I've heard that Marshall is a black belt. I've never met a black belt before! Are you a black belt, too?" asked Nero.

"I am! Now you know two black belts! I hear that you're a great artist! What kind of art do you do?" asked Art.

"I draw and paint. You know, whatever comes to my head. No two designs are ever alike. I guess you could say that I like to work on a large canvas whenever possible," explained Nero.

"Maybe you could show us some of your artwork sometime," said Marshall.

"I can show you right now, if you like. I carry my paints with me wherever I go. Let's go to the back of the mall behind the shops," said Nero.

The brothers seemed a little confused because Nero didn't seem to be carrying anything. But they really wanted to see his designs and hang out with the new kid that everyone was talking about.

Once they got behind the shops, Nero lifted up his big, baggy sweatshirt. Strapped on a unique belt around his waist were small, shiny cans of spray paint. He had cans of bright blue, green, yellow, red, and black.

Nero took out the black can, began to shake it, and then pointed it at the wall. Now, Marshall and Art figured out exactly what kind of art Nero did!

"Hey!" yelled Marshall. "What are you doing? You can't spray paint on the wall! Nero, what you do is called graffiti and that makes you a tagger, not an artist. More importantly, it's against the law! You can't paint on other people's property no matter how creative and talented you are!"

17

"Our city has committees that donate their time and hard work to clean up the 'artwork' that you and other taggers put on walls," Art added. "You know, some people actually want their blank walls *blank*! Then, you come along and paint on them and that's not right!"

Nero suddenly got a strange look on his face. "I never looked at it that way before. It seems strange that art would be against the law. I tried to use my talent to make the city more beautiful, that's all. Without my paintings, I'm just like everyone else. Even my name is boring and plain, like me," mumbled Nero.

"What are you talking about? We've never met anyone from France before and your name is the most unusual name I've ever heard. Nero Stomel sounds cool, if you ask me," said Marshall.

"My name is not Nero Stomel. My real name is Oren Lemots. I didn't like 'Oren' so I go by Nero. It's Oren backward. And I'm not from France either. I'm from just across town," sighed Oren.

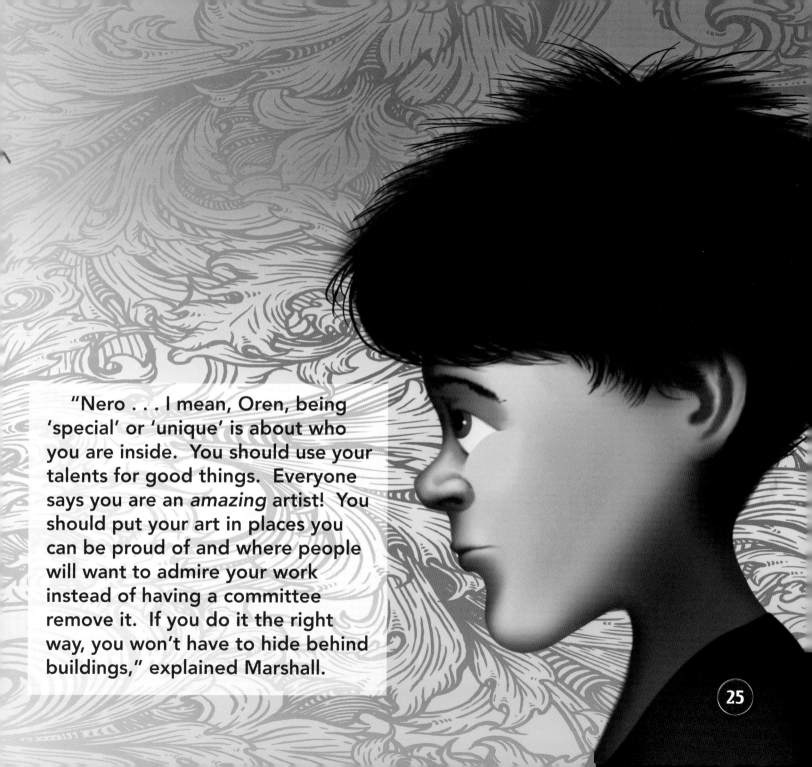

"Nero . . . I mean, Oren, being 'special' or 'unique' is about who you are inside. You should use your talents for good things. Everyone says you are an *amazing* artist! You should put your art in places you can be proud of and where people will want to admire your work instead of having a committee remove it. If you do it the right way, you won't have to hide behind buildings," explained Marshall.

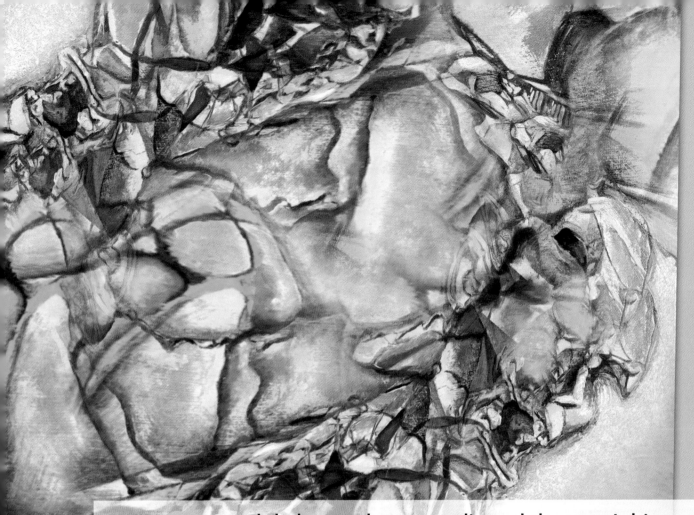

"My mom and dad own a karate studio and the town's biggest art gallery owner, Ollie Farfallee, is one of their students. I bet Mr. Farfallee would love to see your artwork and then he can tell you what he thinks. On a canvas or in a frame that is, *not* on a building! You could become a famous artist someday, Oren!" said Marshall excitedly.

"You'd do that for me?" asked Oren. "Wow, just think . . . my paintings hanging in a real art gallery! That would be way cool! I could show people my artwork without having to take them to a warehouse wall or to the back of an office building!" marveled Oren.

"Yeah, and you wouldn't have to hide from the sheriff either! You haven't put your designs on the police station, yet, have you?" teased Art.

Oren felt pretty lucky to have run into Marshall and Art. "Do you guys know if there is a place I can write to so I can make up for the damage I've done? I want to help clean up the messes I've made."

The brothers couldn't wait to tell their mom and dad all about Oren. Maybe someday Oren's paintings might actually be hanging in an art gallery thanks to Marshall and Art!

Tips for Avoiding Peer Pressure

Marshall and Art know breaking the law isn't cool. Here are some tips for standing up for doing the right thing:

Children:
- When your friends are "cool," that doesn't mean that whatever they do is cool, too. If you see or learn of someone doing something that isn't right, it's ok to be the one that stands up and says so.
- Don't let friends or anyone persuade you to keep secrets. Usually if someone needs you to keep a secret, it's not for a good reason. Never keep a secret from your parents! Share with your parents, teachers, or counselors anything that doesn't feel right to you.
- Encourage your friends to use their energy for positive things that they can feel good about. A friend who doesn't do the right things may not be the kind of friend you want after all.

Adults:
- Check out your kids' rooms once in a while. Closed doors prevent proper supervision. Privacy is one thing, secrecy is another.
- Kids are often tempted to keep secrets or ask their friends to share in a secret. Encourage children from time to time to remain open with you or another adult they trust about anything they sense isn't right.
- Young children often aren't aware of things that are considered "illegal" such as graffiti, use of firecrackers, or spray paints as an accelerant. So, as children get older, take the time to discuss certain childhood temptations and how to avoid common peer pressure.